Bess

Two Colorful Tales

ART LESSONS BY BESS

AND

A MASTERPIECE FOR BESS

RANDOM HOUSE 🏠 NEW YORK

Art Lessons by Bess

WRITTEN BY
AMY VINCENT

ILLUSTRATED BY
JUDITH HOLMES CLARKE,
MERRY CLINGEN, DEE FARNSWORTH,
ADRIENNE BROWN & CHARLES PICKENS

RANDOM HOUSE 🏠 NEW YORK

"JUST A SMIDGE more yellow—that's it!"

Bess fluttered back from her latest painting to get a better look. Her studio was, as usual, a mess. Open tubes of paint lay on her table, and the cloths she used to wipe her hands were stained with dozens of yellow fingerprints. But Bess didn't see any of that. While she was hard at work on a painting, she had eyes for nothing else.

This particular painting was very special to Bess, who was Pixie Hollow's busiest art-talent fairy. Although she often painted portraits or still lifes, she liked to experiment. Other fairies didn't always understand her more abstract paintings. But Bess loved the freedom of expressing herself this way.

Slowly Bess turned upside down in midair. Her brown hair dangled upon her palette. A few strands fell into the paint, but Bess didn't notice.

She was deep in thought when she was startled by a voice.

"Bess!" Lily, a garden-talent fairy, appeared at the door of Bess's tangerine-

crate studio. "Did you hear?"

Bess, embarrassed to have been caught behaving oddly, quickly fluttered right side up again. Too late, she glimpsed the yellow paint in her hair and quickly brushed it away from her face.

Lily didn't seem to have noticed.

"Big news," she said. "A laugh is coming. You know what that means!"

"An arrival!" Bess clapped her hands. "How exciting!"

Every time a baby laughed for the first time, the laugh floated straight to Never Land. There, the laugh turned into a brand-new fairy or a sparrow man. Each arrival was cause for celebration. New arrivals meant new friends. They also meant a friendly kind of contest between all the different talent groups of fairies. Each talent group always wanted another member. The light-talent fairies needed help catching sunbeams, and the mining talent fairies needed help digging. The cooking-talent fairies always hoped for someone else to bake muffins, and the water-talent fairies were eager to teach their best charms.

Naturally, Bess hoped the new fairy would be an art-talent fairy. She hurriedly wiped her hands and went to join Lily. She left her mess behind her. But who could worry about that? An arrival was coming!

At the lagoon, a crowd had gathered. Fairies and sparrow men laughed and hugged one another. It felt almost like a party.

Lily and Bess landed in the middle of the group. Leo, an art-talent sparrow man whose specialty was painting murals, waved to them. "Do you think we'll get a new art-talent fairy this time?"

he asked Bess. "We haven't had anyone in ages. It's our turn!"

"I wouldn't mind having somebody else to enjoy the gardens with," Lily said.

"The island's magic knows best," Bess said firmly.

"Look!" cried light-talent fairy Fira, blazing brightly as she darted above the others. "Here it comes!"

A tiny shimmer of light flickered overhead. Bess felt the air shiver with anticipation. The laugh fluttered downward, shifting from blue to pink to purple. It burst open to reveal a flash of sparkles—and a brand-new fairy!

She blinked several times, as if in surprise. The new fairy was very tiny, and she had thick, messy, curly hair in the

brightest shade of red Bess had ever seen.

At this point, most new arrivals stepped forward and introduced themselves. But the new fairy did not. Instead she stood where she had landed, twirling a lock of red hair around her fingers.

Everyone looked at each other in confusion. Fira, who had taken care of new fairies before, asked kindly, "Can you tell us who you are?"

"I—I think I can." The new fairy scratched the side of her head. Then the answer came to her. "My name is Scarlett!"

Fira smiled in encouragement. "Welcome to Pixie Hollow, Scarlett."

"It's good to be home!" Scarlett paused. "This *is* my new home, isn't it?"

"Of course it is," said Fira as she took Scarlett's hand.

Bess, along with all the others, murmured her encouragement. Apparently the trip to Never Land had confused Scarlett a bit! But that was all right. Lots of fairies weren't sure how to behave at first.

Fira said, "Tell us, Scarlett—what is your talent?"

All the fairies and sparrow men leaned closer, eager to hear the answer.

"I'm an art-talent fairy," Scarlett said.

All the art-talent fairies cheered, and Bess hurried forward with the others to greet her. "How wonderful!" said Quill, an art-talent fairy who worked as a sculptor. "We're so glad you're one of us."

"Pixie Hollow is a wonderful place to create art," Leo explained. "I work on murals of the landscape. Bess here paints all kinds of beautiful pictures. Quill carves amazing statues. Whatever you want to do here, you'll find all the help you need."

Bess asked, "So what is it that you do, Scarlett? Are you a painter, like me? What kind of art will you create?"

Scarlett thought for a moment before she shrugged. "I have no idea."

Bess and Quill looked at each other, confused. How could Scarlett not know what kind of art-talent she had? Most fairies knew precisely what their specialties were from the moment they first arrived.

"What's the matter?" Scarlett asked innocently. She began picking up twigs from the ground and twirling them into her hair. The twigs stuck out in every direction. "Is something wrong?"

"Of course not," Bess said, but she didn't quite mean it. Scarlett didn't know her specialty, and she seemed to behave oddly.

There was no other way to say it: The new fairy was *weird*.

"How can Scarlett not know what sort of art she's interested in?" Quill whispered. She and Bess were huddled with the other art-talent fairies at the edge of the lagoon. Scarlett, still wearing her Arrival Garment, kept picking up seashells and trying them on as hats.

Bess's glow blushed pink with embarrassment for Scarlett. Of course, Scarlett didn't seem ashamed of her odd behavior.

Scarlett seemed even stranger because she didn't know her own artistic specialty. Most fairies knew as soon as they arrived. Bess had emerged already eager to hold a paintbrush for the first time. She remembered when Jax, a glass-blowing-talent sparrow man, first arrived in Pixie Hollow. He had asked to be taken to the glassworks even before he had told anyone his name!

At last Scarlett noticed that everyone was watching her. "Am I doing something wrong?" she asked cheerfully. A pink shell slipped from her head into the sand.

"Of course not," Leo said. He put a reassuring hand on her shoulder. "It's simply that—that—" Bess knew he wanted to ask about Scarlett's funny behavior, but instead he stuck to what was simpler. "You see, most of us arrive knowing what kind of art we like."

"Not everybody!" said Jolie, a papier-mâché-talent fairy. "I didn't figure it out for almost five whole minutes. So you just wait. The answer will come to you."

"I bet you figure out your specialty once you get your magic," Bess said. "Terence, come and help us!"

"On my way!" cried Terence, a dust-talent sparrow man. It was Terence's job to scatter pixie dust, which gave fairies their magic and allowed them to fly.

Terence flew over Scarlett and scattered a teacup of shimmering pixie dust over her. Scarlett held out her hands and twirled in the sparkling powder.

"There you go," Bess said as Scarlett flapped her wings for the first time. "Now you can fly!"

"Oh, this is wonderful!" Scarlett cried as she rose into the air. She rose up, up, up—

CRASH!

She smacked her head into a tree branch.

"Ow!" yelped all the fairies. Scarlett hovered unevenly. Terence quickly went to her side and steadied her as they lowered to the ground.

"Are you all right?" Terence asked.

He looked at Scarlett and frowned. "I think you got some twigs in your hair when you hit the tree."

"Oh, no, I put them there! I thought they would keep my curls out of my face," Scarlett said. She re-twisted the knot of hair at the back of her head. "It's comfortable, too. How does it look?"

"It's—um—" Bess struggled to find the right words. "Well, it's very original!"

Quill whispered, "We've got to get her to the coiffure-talent fairies!"

Scarlett finished doing up her hair with a smile. "What do we do next?"

The other fairies and sparrow men all glanced at each other. Usually, new art-talent fairies wanted to start creating art right away.

But Scarlett still didn't know what kind of art she would create. She was the only art-talent fairy who had ever gone so long without knowing.

That meant nobody really knew what to do with her.

"I know," Bess said. "Let's take a look at your new room in the Home Tree. The decoration-talent fairies should have it ready by now."

"A room all for me?" Scarlett brightened. "I'd love to see it!"

Cheered, everyone zipped into the air and flew with Scarlett over Pixie Hollow. As they went, the fairies pointed out different places she needed to recognize: the lagoon, the mines, Lily's garden.

The art-talent fairies all lived in the same area of the Home Tree, and there was a branch they usually landed upon. Everyone descended gracefully—except Scarlett. She wobbled a little, unsure of her balance.

"Don't worry!" she called, pinwheeling her arms around. "I've got it!" Somehow Scarlett managed not to fall.

When they arrived, they discovered that the decorating-talent fairies had outdone themselves. The walls were robin's-egg blue, and Scarlett's silver, oval-shaped bed was piled high with soft pillows.

"It's so beautiful," Scarlett said as she stroked the milky-white drapes. "This is really all for me?"

Bess nodded. She, along with Jolie and Quill, were touring the room, too. "Usually the decorating-talent fairies put something on the walls, but not for us. They know that we'll create our own art soon enough. And we always like our own work best."

"Even if nobody else does!" joked Quill. They all laughed.

"And these clothes?" Scarlett threw open the closet door. "They're all for me?"

"The sewing-talent fairies are truly wonderful," Jolie said. Happily, she smoothed the skirt of her lilac-colored dress. "Which reminds me—are those new leggings, Quill? They're very nice!"

"Thank you," Quill said with a smile.

Nobody said anything about Bess' clothes, which were smudged with paint. Bess edged behind the footboard of Scarlett's bed, hoping the others wouldn't notice.

They didn't—because they were looking at Scarlett.

Scarlett had discarded her arrival garment and slipped on a bright turquoise skirt—but she was wearing it as a shirt. The hem didn't quite reach her knees. Now she had a long green stocking on one leg and was putting a blue-and-white striped stocking on the other.

"You know, Scarlett, those socks don't quite match, Bess pointed out."

"Who wants to wear only one color when you can wear them all at once?" Scarlett grinned, proud of her strange outfit.

None of the others knew quite what to say. Quickly, Jolie clasped her hands together. "So, Scarlett, have you realized your special talent yet?"

Scarlett shook her head. "You'll help me think of it, right?"

Bess put one hand on Scarlett's shoulder. "We'll figure it out together," she said. "You'll see!"

3

EVERY EVENING, THE residents of Pixie Hollow gathered together for dinner. The cooking-talent fairies prided themselves on creating delicious meals even for ordinary days. However, when they had heard about the new arrival, they had made the night's meal even more special.

The long tables for each talent group were decorated with wreaths of soft clover. Acorn soup simmered in pots, and huckleberry tarts waited beside every plate. As Bess and Scarlett flew into the tearoom, Bess's mouth began to water.

"This feeling in my tummy—" Scarlett put her hands on her belly. One of the twigs behind her ear stuck out at an odd angle. "Does this mean—am I— *hungry?*"

Bess swiftly explained, "Yes, you're hungry. It's dinnertime. This is where we all eat together, see?" She realized people must be staring at Scarlett's odd outfit.

"This room is amazing." Scarlett pointed upward. "See how the ceiling curves? That catches the light and makes everything seem taller."

Bess raised an eyebrow, surprised and impressed. Only an art-talent fairy would notice that kind of detail about the tearoom.

Bess wanted to sit down to her meal like everyone else. Her belly was rumbling with hunger already. But Scarlett didn't budge. She kept turning around in a circle, admiring the tearoom.

"Scarlett? Don't you want to eat?" Bess asked.

"Oh, that's right—I'm hungry!" Scarlett smiled brightly at Bess, who couldn't help smiling back.

They headed toward the art-talent group table. Already the serving-talent fairies had begun flying to each place, pouring elderberry juice from pitchers. In fact, Scoop, one of the serving-talent sparrow men, was headed their way. Scarlett, who wasn't looking where she was going, fluttered into Scoop's path.

"Watch out!" Bess cried. But she was too late to keep them from colliding.

Both Scarlett and Scoop tumbled to the floor. Elderberry juice splashed everywhere. Scoop scowled as he rubbed his sore head, and Scarlett lay sprawled on the floor. Juice dripped from her hair and wings. "I'd fly backward if I could!" she said to Scoop. That was what fairies said instead of "I'm sorry."

"That's all right," Scoop replied, though he looked a little grumpy. "We have plenty more juice in the kitchens."

Bess picked up the pitcher. "See, this didn't break. It's fine."

A few fairies giggled, but more helped dry Scoop and Scarlett. Soon everyone began eating and chatting again. "That's a relief," Bess said. "Nobody's staring anymore!"

"Were they staring?" Scarlett didn't even seem to mind the juice stain on her outfit. "I didn't notice."

"Don't worry about it," Bess said.

But she couldn't help thinking that maybe it was time to worry about Scarlett a little bit.

Scarlett was klutzy. She wore weird clothes and had an even weirder hairstyle. The others were sure to laugh at her. Wouldn't they laugh even harder when they realized Scarlett still didn't know her specialty?

The only fairy who had ever taken so long to realize her unique skill was Prilla, who could appear to Clumsy children so that they believed in fairies. Prilla's talent was one-of-a-kind, which was why nobody had known. Art talent wasn't like that. Scarlett really should know her specialty by now.

Once they finally began eating with the others, Bess relaxed. Peculiar as Scarlett was, she was definitely friendly—and smart, too.

For instance, as Scarlett listened avidly, Leo described his latest work in progress, a mural of the seashore. Then

she said, "How fascinating. You must have trouble with the water, though— it's so much blue. Does it overwhelm the rest of the painting?"

"Sometimes," Leo admitted. "I've varied the shades, from baby blue to indigo, and that helps. But I keep thinking it needs something more."

Scarlett tilted her head to one side as she considered it. One of the twigs slipped loose from her hair and clattered to the floor, but Scarlett didn't seem to notice. "Have you considered painting a windy day, instead of a calm one?"

Leo snapped his fingers. "Of course! If the sea is choppy, then the waves will be white with foam. That will make the whole mural more interesting. Great idea, Scarlett!"

The other art-talent fairies grinned. Nobody even made a face when Scarlett picked up the fallen twig and twisted it back into her hair. She definitely had the instincts of an artist, that was certain.

As the serving-talent fairies took the empty plates away after dinner, Scarlett and Bess rose from the table. "You must be tired after your first day," Bess said.

"I feel too excited to sleep." Scarlett hugged herself. "It's just so beautiful here! Why, look at these clover chains—that pale green is gorgeous!"

With that, Scarlett grabbed a clover chain and picked it up. She probably only meant to encourage Bess to take a closer look. But when she pulled the clover chain, it snaked across the table. The chain tangled around the glasses and plates, pulling them from their places—toward the edge of the table, until they fell.

The glasses and dishes smashed to the floor, scattering into dozens of pieces.

"Oh, no!" Scarlett cried.

"It's okay." Scoop hurried over, ready to clean up. "People break glasses every so often."

Bess's glow blushed as brightly as Scarlett's red hair.

Scarlett didn't blush. She said to Scoop, "Are you sure you aren't mad?"

Scoop sighed, then smiled. "No, I'm not. It's sort of funny, now that I think about it." He laughed, and Scarlett did, too.

Some fairies had already left the tearoom, but many remained and had seen the whole thing. Bess could hear the whispers:

"The new one certainly is awkward!"

"Poor thing."

"I wouldn't want her near anything I was working on."

Bess put her arm around Scarlett's shoulders. "First thing tomorrow, you should come to my studio," Bess said loudly. "We'll see if you have a feel for painting."

"That sounds great." Scarlett looked perfectly happy. Bess smiled uncomfortably, trying to remember all the fragile things in her studio she'd need to hide away before tomorrow.

4

BESS GLANCED AROUND her tangerine-crate studio. As usual, it was quite untidy. Paints and brushes lay everywhere. Stray canvases were stacked in every corner.

As soon as she tucked her last glass jar behind some old blankets, she heard a rap on the side of the crate.

"Bess? Are you there?"

"Hi, Scarlett. Welcome to my studio."

Scarlett came inside. Scarlett's eyes lit up as she saw Bess's red and gold abstract painting. "Did you do that? It's beautiful. So emotional!"

"That's what I'm working on now." Bess admitted, "Most people don't like my abstract pictures."

"It reminds me of a rose," Scarlett said. "I think it's marvelous."

Bess smiled. The praise pleased her, and she now knew Scarlett had very good taste. *Maybe she'll turn out to be a painter after all!* she thought.

Scarlett asked, "Will we be working on that painting today?"

"I thought we might try something

different. Let's stretch our canvases and get the paints," Bess said. "We'll have to be ready to begin before Fawn gets here."

As they stretched white canvas over frames, Scarlett said, "How will Fawn be helping us?"

"Recently I've wanted to paint a portrait of a baby animal. So I asked Fawn to find a willing model. She's an animal-talent. She should be here any moment."

"Baby animals are adorable," Scarlett said, watching as Bess smeared several paints upon a palette. Then she began doing the same herself. "Oh, I hope I'm a painter!"

As they finished preparing, Bess

heard Fawn call, "Hello there!"

"Fawn! We've been waiting for you!" Bess hurried to the door of her studio. "Who have you brought for us to paint?—Oh!"

To Bess's dismay, Fawn stood at the door with a baby skunk.

"Here's your model, Bess!" Fawn announced cheerfully.

"Yes, but—a skunk? He won't—" Bess pinched her nose with two fingers and waved her other hand in front of her!

"Oh, no, he'll be fine," Fawn insisted. "Skunks only spray when they're frightened. You won't scare him, will you?"

"I think he's lovely," Scarlett said.

"The contrast of black and white in his fur should look very striking in the painting."

That's true, Bess thought. She smiled gently at the little skunk. The skunk scampered into the studio, ready to pose.

"Look at him," Fawn giggled. "He's flattered!"

The little skunk had fluffed his tail. He turned his head this way and that, trying to look more handsome.

"Perfect," Scarlett said. "Hold it just there! You look great."

The tiny skunk preened.

Bess got to work right away. She sat at her easel, and Scarlett sat at hers, a few feet away. Fawn hovered several steps behind them, watching them work and keeping the baby skunk company.

Soon Bess was too absorbed in her painting to notice what the others were doing.

A few shadows here—maybe a little white there—Bess stuck the tip of her tongue out of her mouth, the way she often did when concentrating. Then hurriedly she pulled it back in. She didn't want to appear silly in front of the others!

"Scarlett?" Bess said, still looking at her own canvas. "How are you doing?"

"Um." Scarlett paused, and then repeated, "Um."

Bess turned from her painting to look at Scarlett's. Her heart sank.

Although Bess's painting was hardly more than a few lines on the canvas, the shape was clearly that of a skunk. Scarlett's painting didn't look like a skunk. It didn't look like much of anything. All Scarlett could paint was a scribble. And not even a black and white scribble!

Fawn flew a little closer and frowned. "Is that supposed to be a dragonfly? I can bring one here, if you want."

"That's all right, Fawn. We're fine," Bess said quickly. She was worried about the disappointed look on Scarlett's face. Thinking fast, she suggested, "Maybe you should try something abstract. Like the painting of mine you liked so much."

Scarlett brightened. "That's a good idea. I can just—swirl the paint around."

Bess felt more hopeful as she turned back to her own work. The little skunk was still posing perfectly. She said to Fawn, "Tell your friend that he's a wonderful model."

Fawn spoke to the skunk. What she said sounded to Bess like so much chirping and humming. The baby skunk brightened and arched his tail to look even prettier.

Scarlett smiled.

The skunk's face smiled back from Bess's canvas. She still had much to do, but this was progress. Bess called, "How does yours look, Scarlett?"

"I'm not sure," Scarlett said weakly.

Bess turned to see Scarlett's canvas. She had smeared paint all over it, but it didn't look anything like Bess's abstract work. Instead, the painting looked like a big blur.

Scarlett said, "I think I'm not a painter."

"You can't be sure yet," Bess insisted. "Let your feelings go. Express yourself! Go wild! Get lost in emotion!"

"Okay." Scarlett squeezed a large blob of yellow paint onto her palette. She took a deep breath as she scooped it up in her fingers. "Emotion. Wild. Right—now!"

Scarlett threw the yellow paint toward the canvas. It spattered brightly.

"Well," Fawn said, "I guess that looks cheerful."

"Cheerful!" Scarlett bounced up and down, getting excited. "So now some—blue!"

Blue paint went *splat* onto the canvas. This, too, looked cheerful—but it clashed with the yellow, in Bess's opinion.

Scarlett frowned. She'd seen it too. "I need something to tie the colors together, don't I? What about—green?"

"It's worth a try," Bess said.

Quickly Scarlett grabbed a tube of green and squeezed a huge glob of it into her hand. She swirled her hand around and closed her eyes, muttering, "Be wild. Wild. Wild!"

Without opening her eyes, Scarlett threw the green paint as hard as she could.

Except that she missed the canvas.

Bess gasped as paint splattered all over the baby skunk. The skunk, startled, lifted his tail and—

"Oh, no!" all three fairies cried as skunk-stink filled the studio. Bess and

Scarlett ran outside for fresh air, coughing. Fawn remained inside to calm the little skunk.

"Is he okay?" Scarlett cried to Fawn. "I didn't mean to scare him!"

"He'll be fine," Fawn said. Through the window, Bess could see Fawn petting the skunk's head. "He's mostly embarrassed."

Bess sighed. "Don't feel bad, Scarlett. That could have happened to anyone."

"At least we know one thing," Scarlett said. "We know I'm not a painter."

5

AFTER FAWN HAD taken the baby skunk
back home, Bess and Scarlett hovered
outside the studio, unsure what to do.
The entire tangerine create stank of
skunk.

"What will I tell everyone?" Bess
said. The other fairies were sure to think
this was ridiculous.

Scarlett said, "Tell them the truth, of course—that I frightened the skunk. I'd fly backward if I could, Bess. I know this leaves you without a place to work."

"That's all right," Bess said. She felt like she could use a couple of days to recover. "I just wish I knew when I could use my studio again."

"Only a couple of days," cried a voice from overhead, "if you let me help you!"

Bess and Scarlett looked up. Above them, Lily hovered in the air, holding a tomato so plump her arms could hardly fit around it. "Why do you have a tomato?" Bess said in surprise.

"The best way to remove skunk-stink is with tomato juice." Lily nodded firmly. "Trust me. This is exactly what your studio needs."

Scarlett smiled in delight. "Really? How does it work?"

Lily explained, "We're going to squash tomatoes in Bess's studio. We'll make a big mess, but the juice will take the smell away. Then Rani has promised to rinse everything clean with some water charms."

"It's that simple?" Bess felt relieved. "Are you sure you both have time to help?"

"It's the least I can do, after frightening the skunk," Scarlett said.

Lily giggled. "I'm glad to help, but really, I just think squashing tomatoes is fun. Watch!"

With that, Lily flew to the door of Bess's studio, dropped the tomato at the open doorway, and jumped down upon it. Brilliant red juice sprayed in every direction—and all over Lily.

Everyone began to laugh. Lily looked so silly, with tomato juice dripping from her hair and her nose.

Oh, dear—will I look like that, too? Bess didn't like looking ridiculous in front of her friends. Yet she realized that already the smell wasn't so bad. It was going to work!

If it would make her studio usable again, Bess was willing to do anything, even look silly.

For the next couple of hours, Bess, Lily, and Scarlett worked together. They

would fly to Lily's garden to gather
tomatoes, then back to the tangerine-
crate studio. Each fairy would put a
tomato on the floor, fly up to the
ceiling, and then—SPLAT! SPLAT!
SPLAT!

They squashed each tomato, flying
downward in belly flops and swan dives.

The smell improved bit by bit.

Scarlett and Lily seemed to be having the time of their lives. Neither one paid any attention to the red juice and pulp all over their clothes and skin. Bess couldn't relax, knowing that she was the messiest she'd ever been in her life. But she kept working hard.

After they'd squashed the last tomato, Scarlett said, "Is that it?" She sounded disappointed that the fun ever had to stop.

"Afraid so," Lily said. "You'll want to let the studio air out for the rest of the day, Bess."

"That's okay," Bess said. "I'm just glad it will be all right."

"There must be so many interesting uses for the plants in your garden, Lily."

Scarlett looked thoughtful. "Tomatoes get rid of skunk-stink. Who would have guessed? What else can you tell me?"

Lily's eyes lit up. Bess knew that Lily didn't talk much—but when she began chatting about her garden, she could go on for quite a while.

Quickly Bess said, "I'm going to go clean up, if that's okay with you."

"That's fine," Lily said, taking Scarlett's hand. "The two of us have plenty to talk about."

Bess flew to a nearby stream to wash up. She didn't want everyone in Pixie Hollow to see her while she was stained tomato red from head to toe. It took her a long time and a lot of scrubbing before she felt presentable again.

By the time she returned to her studio, Lily and Scarlett had left.

Now, where might Scarlett have gone? Bess wondered. She could simply have gone back to her own room in the Home Tree. But that didn't seem much like Scarlett. She would rather be out exploring.

Bess decided to visit the other art-talent fairies. Chances were that Scarlett would be with one of them.

Once her wings were dry, she flew to Quill's sculpture studio, and realized she was right. Through the window she saw Quill and Scarlett sitting together.

"Hello!" Bess called. "Scarlett, I was looking for you! You wandered off!"

Scarlett held a hand to her forehead,

as if in distress. "I'm surprised you want to see me after what I did. Ruining your studio!"

Bess could tell that Scarlett was joking, but Quill couldn't. Like many art-talent fairies who specialized in sculpture, Quill could be stubborn as a rock sometimes.

"I told Scarlett that wasn't her fault!" Quill said to Bess. Her eyes flashed as she looked at Bess.

Bess smiled, hoping to set Quill at ease. "Scarlett's just joking. Lily knew how to clean the scent out. In a couple of days, my studio will be as good as new."

Scarlett brightened. "Oh, good!"

Reassured, Quill settled back into the conversation. "Scarlett and I were just talking about my mermaid statue."

Sitting in the corner was the mermaid. Quill had carved it last year, and every fairy in Pixie Hollow agreed it was her greatest statue yet. The limestone mermaid seemed to be leaping from the water. Quill had etched every curl of her hair and every scale of her tail.

"Tell her what you said, Scarlett," Quill whispered.

Scarlett pointed at the mermaid's arched tail. "See how her fins curve? The statue really seems to move."

Once again, Bess was impressed. Scarlett certainly had artistic instincts, even if she couldn't paint!

Quill said, "She sounds like a

sculptor to me."

"Could be." Bess nodded.

"I know just the thing!" Quill ran to her supply cupboard. From inside she pulled out a large block of marble the color of a soft pink rose. "This marble is very special," she said. "The mining-talent fairies brought it to me just last week. There's not a single flaw in the stone."

"Look how the surface shines," Scarlett said. "You would hardly have to polish the statue when you were done."

Proudly, Quill held out her chisel and mallet. "Scarlett, I want you to carve the stone."

Scarlett gasped. "Are you sure? Don't you want this for yourself?"

"I want to see what you can do,"

Quill said firmly. Bess nodded.

Slowly, Scarlett took the chisel and mallet. Bess took Quill's hand in anticipation.

"I'm trying to see a shape in the stone," Scarlett said.

"Good!" Quill said.

"A rose, maybe. Or a tulip." Scarlett closed her eyes, as if she were looking for the shape in her mind, instead of the stone.

"You'll see it once you start," Bess said. "Go on, Scarlett, try it!"

Scarlett put the chisel at the very top of the pink marble and took a deep breath. "Here goes," she whispered. Then she brought the mallet down hard.

A jagged line split the entire block

of marble in two! Bess and Quill stared, horrified, as each half of the block tumbled off its pedestal onto the floor.

Quill made a face that would've been funny if Bess hadn't been so embarrassed for Scarlett.

"Oh, no!" Scarlett cried. "I've ruined your marble!"

"You haven't ruined it," Quill said quickly. She knelt to scoop the fallen half into her arms. "Now I can make two smaller statues instead of only one."

Scarlett sighed. "Still, I did everything wrong again. I must not be a sculptor, either."

Bess patted Scarlett's shoulder. "It's okay," she said. "We'll find an answer soon."

Deep down, however, Bess was starting to wonder if they would ever figure out what Scarlett could do right.

"Maybe you should take a break for a while," Bess said as she and Scarlett left Quill's studio. "You've had quite a day."

Scarlett said, "Really, I'd rather keep trying. I want to learn what my talent might be."

They both zoomed into the sky. From above, both Bess and Scarlett could see Pixie Hollow as the busy, magical place that it was. In a small brook, Rani the water-talent fairy swam in the current. She was the only fairy who could swim, as she had no wings to weigh her down. Overhead, Fira the light-talent fairy taught a group of fire-flies a new flight formation.

A group of cooking-talent fairies flew nearby, carrying fruits and vegetables from Lily's garden. Bess could hear one of them asking another, "Where did all the tomatoes go?"

She turned to share the joke with Scarlett. But Scarlett's face was sad.

"Scarlett?" Bess nudged Scarlett toward a nearby maple tree. They perched on the edge of a branch amid the wide

green leaves. "Are you all right?"

"It's just hard to see everyone so busy," Scarlett said. "Each fairy and sparrow man in Pixie Hollow has a talent. They work all day doing what they love. I want that, too."

This was the first time Bess had seen Scarlett being anything less than cheerful. No, it wouldn't do any good to ask Scarlett to rest. They had to keep searching until they found the kind of art Scarlett could create.

Bess realized that they weren't far from Aidan's workshop. That gave her an idea. "Tell me, Scarlett—do you like jewelry?"

"I think so," Scarlett said. She was twisting a brand-new twig in her hair.

"We're going to visit the sparrow man who makes the most important jewelry of all," Bess said. "Queen Clarion's crown!"

"Jewelry-making talent?" said Aidan. "Well, it's worth a try."

Bess, Scarlett, and Aidan all stood in the middle of Aidan's workshop. The workshop was a cozy little place, comfortably cluttered with metal and tools. One of the queen's golden bracelets lay on his workbench, waiting to be fixed. In the big fireplace, a roaring blaze warmed the whole room.

"Aidan is Pixie Hollow's only crown-repair-talent sparrow man," Bess explained to Scarlett. "He fixes all kinds of jewelry, not only the queen's crown. That means he works with gold and silver more than most fairies do. He isn't an art-talent sparrow man himself, but he helps the jewelry-making talent fairies by sharing precious metals."

Scarlett nodded. "I understand. He could teach me about working with the metal, even if we do different things with it. Right?"

"Exactly," Aidan said. He pointed to a small bar of silver sitting on his work bench. "The mining-talent fairies brought this yesterday. Would you like me to melt a bit for you? You could try making a chain, or a ring."

The idea clearly appealed to Scarlett.

Still, she hesitated. "I wouldn't—I couldn't—break the silver, could I?"

Aidan laughed gently. "You can't break silver. Even if it gets dented or scratched, I can always melt it all over again."

Scarlett took a deep breath. "Okay. I'll give it a try."

Swiftly Aidan went to work. He pumped the bellows so that the flames in the fireplace leaped higher. Then he held the silver bar in a pair of tongs and dipped it into the fire. Within seconds, the metal began to melt. Aidan quickly held the bar over a clay plate, and the liquid silver drizzled onto it.

"There," Aidan said. "Let it cool for a few seconds."

As Bess and Scarlett watched, the liquid silver started to take form. Scarlett picked up one of Aidan's tools and prodded a corner of the silver puddle. She managed to nudge the silver into something like a shape.

"That's it!" Bess said. "That's how you start."

Encouraged, Scarlett started to mold the silver. Bess's excitement instantly vanished. Scarlett wasn't creating a ring, a bracelet, or any other sort of jewelry. She only managed to nudge the metal into a roundish sort of saucer.

Without looking up, Scarlett said, "I've got it wrong, haven't I?"

"I'm afraid so," Bess answered quietly.

Everyone was silent for a second.

Then Aidan, trying hard to be cheerful, said, "Well, no harm done."

Scarlett groaned. She walked away from the silver toward the fireplace. Bess followed her. Behind them, Aidan carefully collected the silver.

Scarlett asked, "Bess, are you sure that every art-talent fairy finds her specialty eventually?"

"Absolutely positive," Bess said uncertainly.

"I hope you're right," Scarlett said. "At least this time wasn't a total disaster—whoa!"

She had tripped over one of the pots waiting to be fixed, and fell down sideways onto one end of Aidan's workbench. The other end tilted upward sharply. Everything on the workbench flew up in the air—and Queen Clarion's golden bracelet fell into the fire!

"Oh, no!" Aidan cried. "The queen's bracelet—it's melting!"

"I've got it!" Bess tried to grab the bracelet, but the flames were too hot.

"Don't get burned!" Scarlett pushed past Bess with the tongs. She made a grab at the bracelet with them, but she had never used tongs before. As soon as the bracelet was lifted, it slipped down into the ashes. Soot billowed out, blackening their faces.

"Let me," Aidan said. He took the tongs and quickly fished the bracelet out. It was still in one piece, but some of the fine scrollwork had blurred when the gold had started to melt.

"Oh, no!" Bess cried, coughing. "Scarlett, are you all right? What about you, Aidan?"

"I'm okay," Aidan said.

Scarlett rose from the floor and brushed herself off. "I didn't mean to make such a mess, Aidan."

"That's okay," he said. "I'll have to redo the engraving, but that's just a chance to try something new."

"Looks like I'll have to try something new, too," Scarlett said. Her sooty face was downcast.

Scarlett must be able to create some kind of art, Bess thought. *But can we figure out what it is before she burns Pixie Hollow down?*

7

First thing next morning, Bess started visiting other art-talent fairies to see who might try teaching Scarlett that day.

All the fairies agreed that Scarlett should still explore her creative ability. However, nobody would volunteer to work with her next.

"Glass breaks very easily," Jax said

in the glass-blowing studio. "If she trips into our shelves, she could ruin weeks of our work!"

"I've been working on this seaside mural for more than a month," Leo said. He was painting the choppy waves Scarlett had suggested. "If she made a mistake, it might take me another month to fix it."

"Oh, no," Jolie said, throwing her hands in front of her papier-mâché stars. "Scarlett can't come in here. No, no, no."

Bess sighed in discouragement. She couldn't blame the others for wanting to protect their work. Already she knew she would have to start her baby-skunk portrait over from scratch.

If only there were some safe place for Scarlett to experiment.

Then Bess's face lit up in a smile. She'd had an idea!

What if Scarlett had a studio of her very own? Then she could explore any kind of art she wanted, for as long as she wanted, and nobody else's work would be at risk.

The more Bess thought about the

plan, the more she liked it.

Of course, first she would need a lot of help.

"Everybody—push!"

Bess pushed as hard as she could, along with a half dozen other fairies. Slowly, the pumpkin shell lifted from the ground. They had it!

"This way!" Tinker Bell cried. "Follow me!"

Laughing, Bess and the others began flying the pumpkin shell across the meadow. Above them, Terence showered down a bit of pixie dust to lighten the load.

Bess glanced downward. Fluttering

beneath them were several cooking-talent fairies, each carrying a pot of scooped-out pumpkin. Tonight everyone would share pumpkin muffins!

They had selected the perfect place for Scarlett's new studio—a shady glen not far from Bess's tangerine crate. The fairies settled the pumpkin shell beneath an elm tree.

"Perfect," Tink said as she picked up her saw. "What this studio needs now is a door and some windows."

As Tinker Bell cut a door and windows into the pumpkin shell, other fairies worked on projects to help. The weaving-talent fairies wove a soft hammock for Scarlett to rest in. Fira enchanted a lantern that would burn throughout the night, as brightly or as softly as Scarlett wished. All the art-talent fairies brought different supplies, so Scarlett could try each kind of art in turn.

When they were almost done, Lily said, "One more charm, and we'll have the perfect studio. Ready?"

Everybody nodded. Lily flew over the pumpkin shell, scattering pixie dust. Where it landed, it turned into glitter and made the pumpkin shell hard.

"There!" she said. "Now the pumpkin shell will always stay fresh. Scarlett can use this studio forever."

Bess said, "I can't wait to show her. Come on, let's find Scarlett!"

Everyone raced through Pixie Hollow, calling Scarlett's name. Bess and

Lily found her in Lily's garden.

"I was trying flower arranging," Scarlett said. The flowers she had picked didn't match, however. The colors of the petals clashed as terribly as the clothes she wore. "Looks like that's not my talent, either."

"Oh—my begonias—" Lily put one hand to her mouth. Then she said, "They'll grow back."

Scarlett looked even sadder.

Quickly, Bess said, "Wait until you see what we've made for you!"

They took her hands and flew with her to the pumpkin-shell studio.

"Isn't it wonderful?" Bess cried as she led Scarlett inside. "Look, you can try paints. Varnishes. Engraving.

Anything you want!"

"I can try all by myself," Scarlett said sadly. "Nobody wants to work with me anymore."

Bess and Lily looked at each other, embarrassed. They hadn't realized Scarlett would know why they had built her a studio.

Scarlett quickly added, "But it was so kind of you. Of all of you. And it's the most beautiful studio ever!"

As Bess and Lily left, Bess tried to tell herself that Scarlett would be all right. Surely she would find her specialty now.

But Bess couldn't shake the feeling that Scarlett was even sadder than before.

8

THE NEXT MORNING, Bess stood outside her tangerine-crate studio, waiting hopefully. "Is it ready?" she asked.

"One more wash should do it," Rani answered.

With a wave of Rani's hand, a fountain sprang up inside the studio. Water splashed everywhere! The mist made little rainbows in each window.

Then Rani waved her hand again, and all the water was gone. "Finished!" Rani called. "Now your studio is as good as new."

Bess walked inside, took a deep breath, and smiled. No skunk-stink remained. Her studio smelled fresh and sweet. And it had never been so clean!

I'll mess it up soon enough, Bess thought happily. She was thinking of the brushes and paints she would leave lying around when she got back to work on her pictures.

"You've done a wonderful job, Rani," she said. "It feels good to have everything back to normal."

"I was happy to help," Rani said.

"I'll be going now. I bet you can't wait to start a new painting after taking two whole days off!"

It was tempting to dive back into her work, but there was something else Bess wanted to do. "Actually, I'm going to check on Scarlett first."

Bess waved good-bye to Rani and flew across the glen to Scarlett's pumpkin-shell studio. The orange shell glittered in the midday sun.

"Hello?" Bess called. "Scarlett, are you there?"

"Here I am." Scarlett opened the door of her studio.

"I wanted to see how you were this morning," Bess said. "What have you tried out in your new studio so far?"

"Nothing," Scarlett said.

"Nothing? But—you can try anything here! We brought tons of supplies and books."

"I simply can't stand making another mess right now." Scarlett's glow had dimmed to a flicker, and her wings drooped. Her confidence had been badly hurt during the past few days. "I want to do something I can do well, but I can't imagine what that would be."

Bess thought hard. *Scarlett needs to do something right, so I shouldn't push her toward another talent yet—but it should be something creative.*

She snapped her fingers. "We could use more paint."

Scarlett asked, "More paint?"

"All art-talent fairies have to learn to make paints and plasters. You know, art materials. That's not a talent; that's something we teach each other." Bess smiled.

Scarlett brightened, too. "That must be very important."

"It is! None of us could ever create if the others didn't help make our supplies."

Already, Scarlett was flapping her wings in anticipation. "How do we do that?"

"I'll show you." Bess took Scarlett's hand. "Come on!"

They flew quickly over Pixie Hollow, laughing in the sunshine. Bess knew precisely what to look for, but not where

pull the ivy off the tree, so that the vine and leaves are both attached. The vine is the most important part."

"I understand," Scarlett said. "Let's get started!"

When Scarlett grabbed vines in both hands, Bess quickly said, "Be careful!" But she was a little too late. Scarlett pulled hard, until—

BOING!

The vines snapped back to the tree trunk. Scarlett tumbled backward onto the ground.

"Wow," Scarlett said. "They're very—"

"Stretchy," Bess said.

"And slippery!" Scarlett's hands were shiny with the slick ivy sap.

"We need to pull even harder," Bess explained. "But the vines are so elastic that they're hard to tug free. And of course, they're slippery, so it's easy to lose your grip—"

"Which is when the vines go *boing*!" With determination, Scarlett grabbed a twig that had fallen from her hair and twirled it back into place. "I see how they got the name. Is there any trick to it?"

Bess sighed. "We just have to keep trying until the vine finally pulls free. We'll both fall down a dozen times while we're doing this. It happens to everybody."

That was the part that Bess found most comforting. She didn't mind looking a little silly while collected Boing-Boing Ivy because *everyone* looked silly doing it. Surely Scarlett would be reassured, too.

But Scarlett didn't need anyone to make her feel better. "Pulling Boing-Boing vines sounds like fun! Let's get started!"

They both grabbed handfuls of ivy. "Just pull slowly," Bess said, tugging the ivy carefully away from the tree.

"I'm trying," Scarlett said, grimacing as she pulled.

Maybe we'd make more progress if I pushed while she pulled, Bess thought. Quickly she slipped beneath the vine so she was on the other side, pushing outward.

"Here we go. Take it easy, and—Oh!"

The ivy slipped from their hands with a BOING! The vine smacked into Bess's tummy and pulled her backward with it. Bess felt herself zooming toward the tree, until—

CRASH!

"Bess?" Scarlett ran to the tree trunk. "Bess, are you okay?"

Bess groaned. She was pinned against the birch tree. "I'm fine! Embarrassed, that's all."

Finally sure that Bess wasn't hurt, Scarlett started to giggle. "You did look funny."

"I bet." Bess laughed as she started to wriggle free. But she couldn't quite tug herself loose from the vines. She pulled and pulled, but she couldn't budge.

Scarlett said, "Bess? Are you sure you're okay?"

Bess gulped. "I'm afraid—I'm afraid I'm stuck!"

9

"You're stuck?" Scarlett clapped her hands to her cheeks. "Oh, no!"

Bess tried one more time to free herself from the vines, but she couldn't budge. The ivy held her firmly against the tree trunk.

"Oh, yes," she said. "I'm stuck."

"Does this happen all the time,

too?" Scarlett asked.

"No," Bess admitted. "I think I'm the first fairy who ever managed to tie herself up with the ivy."

She thought about what it would be like when Scarlett went for help. The others would set her free, but oh, they would laugh! They wouldn't mean to be unkind, but who could help laughing at something like this?

Scarlett's eyes widened as she looked at Bess's face. "Are you embarrassed? You shouldn't be. You were only trying to show me what to do."

Bess's glow turned pink. "I know you're right, but I feel—well, pretty silly."

"Trust me," Scarlett said. Her expression became determined. "It's okay, Bess. I'll take care of it. Nobody else will ever find out."

Scarlett grabbed on to the vines and started pulling. She tugged so hard that her wings beat faster than a humming-bird's. There still wasn't enough room for Bess to wiggle free. Scarlett pulled, and pulled, and pulled, and—

BOING!

She lost her grip and went flying backward. After a couple of loops in the air, Scarlett landed flat on her back in the mud.

"Are you hurt?" Bess asked anxiously.

"I'm fine. What about you? Did it hurt when the vine snapped back?"

Bess shook her head. "Not a bit. Can you still pull now that your wings are all muddy?"

"I can use my feet and hands just fine." Scarlett sprang up as though nothing had happened. "We'll try again. This time, you push against the vines at the same time I pull. Ready?"

"Ready," Bess said.

Scarlett took two fistfuls of vine. "One—two—three!"

Bess pushed as hard as she could. The vines were slippery against her hands. She grimaced, but she kept pushing, and Scarlett kept pulling, until—

BOING!

Scarlett went tumbling head over heels. She somersaulted backward until she landed, facedown, in the mud puddle again.

"Scarlett!" Bess cried.

But Scarlett clambered out of the mud once more. To Bess's astonishment, Scarlett was grinning.

Scarlett held out her arms and feebly beat her mud-heavy wings. "So, how do I look?" She turned that way and this, as though she were modeling the latest creation of the dressmaking fairies. Instead she was only modeling a lot of reddish-brown mud.

"You look—really silly!" Bess started to laugh, and Scarlett joined in. Together they giggled for what seemed like a very long time, peals of laughter ringing in the glade. How ridiculous they both were! But—somehow—they were still having fun.

When they finally stopped laughing, Scarlett wiped happy tears from her eyes. Mud smudged her cheeks. "Okay, let's try again."

"Again?" Bess said. "Don't you think you had better go for help?"

"Only if I have to," Scarlett said. "I really think I can get it myself, if I just give it one more twist."

Bess knew that if she were in Scarlett's place, she would have given up by now. She would have flown to find other fairies right away. And if Scarlett were in her place—stuck against a tree—she wouldn't be embarrassed. Scarlett wasn't a bit scared of looking silly. Maybe she wasn't scared of anything.

Bess wished she could be that brave.

Then she realized: She had just wished to be like Scarlett. Scarlett! The one with no talent! The one who put crazy twigs in her hair and wore strange clothes! Who would want to be like Scarlett?

Bess would, she thought as she watched Scarlett grab the ivy vines once more.

"All right," Scarlett said, bracing her feet against the ground. "This time I'm going to twist the vines at the same time. That might break them. Got it?"

"Absolutely," Bess said. "Let's go!"

Bess pushed with all her might. Scarlett pulled even harder. The ivy vines twisted in her grasp, until—

SNAP!

Bess and Scarlett both fell down into

the mud puddle as the vines gave way. Together they laughed even harder than they had before.

"Look at all these vines!" Scarlett held up a handful of Boing-Boing Ivy. "How much do we need for paint?"

"We've got more than enough now," Bess said proudly. "All because of you."

"I didn't do much of anything," Scarlett said.

"You did the most important thing." Bess put one muddy hand on Scarlett's shoulder. "You refused to give up."

Scarlett's eyes twinkled with hope. "First thing tomorrow, I'm going to start experimenting again. This time I won't stop until I find my talent. No matter what."

"Tomorrow?" Bess said. "Not today?"

Scarlett nodded toward the ivy. "Today, I'm making paint for Leo's mural."

Bess beamed. She pulled herself out of the reddish mud and held out a hand to Scarlett. "Need me to help you up?"

"I can manage," Scarlett said. She sighed. "Seems like a shame, though."

"What do you mean?" asked Bess, confused.

"Getting out of all this lovely mud." Scarlett squished some of the mud between her fingers. "It feels so wonderfully goopy. Like I'd love to play in it all day. Don't you feel the same?"

Bess gasped and clapped her hands to her cheeks. The ivy leaves fell in the mud, forgotten for a moment. "Scarlett! I'm not sure, but maybe—just maybe—"

"What?" Scarlett asked.

With a smile, Bess said, "I think I might know what kind of art you should create!"

TOGETHER BESS AND Scarlett raced through Pixie Hollow. Their wings were too muddy for them to fly, but fairies could run quickly when they wanted to. Bess was definitely in a hurry today!

"Where are we going?" Scarlett asked.

"To the pottery workshop!"

The Pixie Hollow pottery workshop

was in a hollowed-out stump not far from Mother Dove's nest. As they swooped downward, Bess and Scarlett saw fairies and sparrow men in aprons, setting out trays of beautiful clay jugs and plates. Other art-talent fairies— mostly painters, like Bess—gathered there, eager to decorate the new creations.

"Hello there!" Bess called as they hurried up. "I was wondering—could Scarlett try making pottery?"

She saw the painting-talent fairies glance at each other. Scarlett had a reputation for disasters. A few people even edged between Scarlett and the new pots, afraid she might knock them over.

A pottery-making fairy named Raku

came out of the workshop, smiling. "You think Scarlett might be one of us? That would be lovely. Why do you think so?"

"The mud," Bess explained. She realized that she and Scarlett were still filthy, head to toe.

"When we were out collecting ivy this morning, we fell in the mud, and Scarlett loved it!" Bess said.

Scarlett shrugged. "How could anybody not love mud?"

"That sounds like a potter, all right." Raku gestured to her work apron, which was covered with splatters of clay. *It won't matter that Scarlett's messy here,* Bess thought. *They all are!* "Let's give it a try. Ready, Scarlett?"

Scarlett glanced at the crowd of other fairies standing nearby. Bess would have been embarrassed to try—and fail—in front of them. But Scarlett lifted her chin proudly. "Ready!"

Maybe someday, Bess thought, *I'll be more like Scarlett, and I won't care what other people think, either. I hope so!*

They walked inside the workshop. There, fairies and sparrow men kneaded clay on broad wooden tables. Others carefully used big paddles to slide soft new pots into the blazing kiln that would bake them into hardness.

Over her shoulder, Bess glanced at the other fairies and sparrow men who were crowding into the windows to see how Scarlett would do. When Scarlett walked near a shelf of newly fired pots—thin and breakable—a few fairies gasped.

Yet Scarlett broke nothing. She was sure and steady now that she was in the pottery workshop.

She's really different here, Bess thought. *It's as if Scarlett belongs. I hope it's true!*

Raku brought Scarlett to a small pottery wheel in the corner. "Normally I would give you an apron to protect your dress," Raku said, "but there's not much point, is there?"

Scarlett laughed and pointed at her muddy clothes. "Not today!"

"Here's what you do," Raku explained as she plopped down a hunk of clay in the center of the wheel. "You press on this pedal on the floor with your foot. That makes the wheel spin."

Scarlett pressed once, and the wheel made a lazy circle.

Raku continued, "Then you dampen your fingers and put your hands on either side of the clay—"

"To center it on the wheel," Scarlett said. Her eyes were sparkling with delight. "Then you can start to mold the clay."

"Exactly!" Raku said. "Give it a try."

A few sparrow men and fairies at the windows started whispering to each other. Bess suspected they were still predicting another disaster.

Come on, Scarlett, she thought. *You can do it!*

Scarlett began working the pedal, and right away the wheel began spinning merrily. She dipped her hands in a nearby bowl of water, then took hold of the clay. Immediately the shapeless lump became a perfect cone.

"She has it balanced already!" Raku said. "That's wonderful!"

Right away, Scarlett pressed her fingers into the center of the cone, and as Bess and the others watched, the clay took the shape of a beautiful round bowl.

Everyone at the windows began to clap and cheer.

Scarlett let the wheel spin to a stop. "That was so much fun!" she said. "It felt so—natural! So easy!"

Raku put a hand on her shoulder. "You are definitely a pottery-talent fairy," she said. "I don't even have to tell you what to do next, do I?"

"Next I trim the bottom of the bowl to give it a more pleasing shape," Scarlett said. "And then I fire it in the kiln, to make it hard, and then I give it to my best friend." She grinned at Bess. Bess smiled back.

"Then I paint it the prettiest color I can think of." Scarlett looked at the bunches of ivy they had left at the door of the workshop. "Maybe dark green?"

Bess hugged Scarlett tightly. They got mud all over each other, but for once, Bess didn't mind if everyone saw her get messy. Not one little bit.

This is the end of
ART LESSONS BY BESS.

Turn the page to read
A MASTERPIECE FOR BESS.

A Masterpiece for Bess

WRITTEN BY
LARA BERGEN

ILLUSTRATED BY
THE DISNEY STORYBOOK ARTISTS

RANDOM HOUSE  NEW YORK

1

"EVERYBODY! COME TO my room!"

Tinker Bell flew about the tearoom. In a silvery voice she called out to the fairies and sparrow men gathered around the tables.

Lily and Rosetta, two garden-talent fairies, looked up from their breakfast of elderberry scones.

"What's the hurry, Tink?" asked Lily.

"Bess has just painted my portrait—and you've got to come and see it!" Tinker Bell urged.

Rosetta and Lily looked at each other in surprise. It wasn't every day that Bess painted a new portrait! What was the occasion? they wondered. But before they could ask, Tink had darted out the tearoom door and into the kitchen.

"Let's go," Rosetta said to Lily. They followed Tink through the Home Tree up to her room.

There the fairies packed themselves in wing to wing, like honeybees in a hive. They could see Bess, in her usual paint-splattered skirt, standing at the front of the room. She was hanging a life-size, five-inch painting of Tinker Bell.

"Isn't it amazing?" gushed Tink. She flew up behind Lily and Rosetta and landed with a bounce on her loaf-pan bed.

And indeed it was. Bess's painting was so lifelike, if a fairy hadn't known better, she might have thought there were *two* Tinks in the room. No detail—from the dimples in Tink's cheeks to her woven sweetgrass belt—was overlooked. What Tink loved most about the painting, though, were the gleaming metal objects piled all around her: pots, pans, kettles, and colanders. She felt as if she could almost pull each one out of the painting.

It was a perfect portrait, as everyone could see. Right away the oohs and aahs began to echo off the tin walls of Tink's room.

"It's lovely!" said Lily. "Bess, you've outdone yourself again!"

"You're too kind. Really," Bess said. Her lemon yellow glow turned slightly tangerine as she blushed. As Pixie Hollow's busiest painter, she was used to praise. But she never tired of hearing it.

"It's just what Tink's room needed," added Gwinn, a decoration-talent fairy. She gazed around Tink's metal-filled room.

"What's the occasion?" asked Rosetta.

"Oh, no occasion, really," said Bess. She brushed her long brown bangs out of her violet eyes. "Tink fixed my best palette knife, and I wanted to do something nice in return."

All around her, the fairies murmured

approvingly. Bess felt her heart swell with pride. *This is what art is all about,* she thought. Times like these made her work worthwhile.

"Personally, I don't see what the fuss is for," a thorny voice said above the

din. "Honestly, my little darlings, what's so great about a fairy standing still?"

Bess didn't have to turn around. She knew who the voice belonged to—and so did everybody else. Vidia, the fastest—and by far the meanest—of the fast-flying-talent fairies, came forward.

"Oh, Vidia," Tink said with a groan. "You wouldn't know fine art if it flew up and nipped you on the nose."

"Yeah, don't listen to her, Bess," Gwinn called out.

"It's okay," Bess assured them. "Every fairy is welcome to have her own opinion."

But as she looked at the portrait again, she frowned slightly. It wasn't that Vidia's criticism bothered her. She'd learned long ago to let the spiteful fairy's snide comments roll off her wings like dewdrops. But Vidia's remark had started the wheels in Bess's mind turning.

"You know . . . ," Bess began.

She searched the room for Vidia. But the fairy had already flown away.

" 'You know' what?" asked Tink.

Bess shook her head. She turned to Tink with a sunny grin. "There's a whole day ahead of us!" she said. "I don't know about you fairies, but I've got work to do."

Spreading her wings, she lifted into the air. "Thanks for coming, everyone," she called.

And with a happy wave, Bess zipped off to her studio.

2

Nowhere else did Bess feel as content as she did in her studio.

Most of the art-talent fairies had studios in the lower branches of the Home Tree. But to Bess there never seemed to be quite enough light—or privacy—there to get her work done. Instead, she had made her studio in an old wooden tangerine crate that had washed up onto a shore of Never Land. She had moved the crate (using magic, of course) to the sunniest, most peaceful corner of Pixie Hollow. It had been her home away from home ever since.

Over time, she'd added things to the crate: a birch-bark cabinet to keep her canvases dry, a soapstone sink in which to wash her brushes, and even a twig cot with a thick hummingbird-down quilt to sleep on when she was painting late into the night.

Bess's studio had grown more and more cluttered. It was, in fact, a bit of a mess. She was not one for tidying up. Why put things away, she always wondered, when you were sure to have to pull them out again someday?

As soon as she reached her studio, Bess began to mix her paints. She took a jar of fragrant linseed oil down from a shelf. Next she brought out a gleaming cherrywood box. The box was polished to a mirrorlike shine. Bess's name was carved into the lid. A carpenter-talent fairy had given it to her as a gift many years before. It was still one of her most prized possessions.

Bess lifted the top of the box. She looked down at the rainbow of powdered pigments inside. Of all the things in her studio, these were the ones she treated like gold.

"Hmm," she mused out loud. "Which colors should I mix first? Orange? Indigo? Hmm . . . What is that *smell*?"

Following her nose, Bess turned to find two brown eyes peeking in at her through the slats in the tangerine crate.

"Dulcie?" she said in suprise. "Is that you?"

Visitors to her studio were rare. Bess fumbled with the latch as she opened the door. "What is it?"

"Oh, nothing," said Dulcie sweetly. "I was just passing through the orchard and thought I'd say hi. Oh! And I thought you might like some poppy puff rolls. Fresh out of the oven!"

Dulcie grinned and held up a basket. She lifted a checked linen cloth off the top. The rich scents of butter and tarragon filled Bess's nose. Her mouth began to water.

"Goodness, Dulcie—your famous rolls. You're really too kind!" said Bess, more surprised than ever.

"I thought you'd be hungry," said Dulcie, handing one to Bess. "Especially after working so hard on Tinker Bell's portrait."

Bess took a bite. "*Mmm*," she said. She closed her eyes and let the flaky layers melt on her tongue. "Delicious, Dulcie! This is so unexpected—and very nice of you! If there's anything I can do for you, just let me know."

"Well," replied Dulcie, "if you wanted to do a portrait of me, that would be fine! I guess I could even pose for you right now. Why, I could pose with my rolls! What do you think?

Should I carry the whole basket or just cradle one in my hand like this?"

Bess swallowed what was left of her roll in one surprised gulp.

"Um . . . uh . . . actually," she stammered, "I was just about to . . ."

"I know!" Dulcie exclaimed. "I'll hold a roll in one hand, and the basket in the other! There! Are you getting this, Bess?"

Bess wiped her buttery hands on her skirt. She hadn't planned to paint another portrait. But how could she refuse? And it certainly was flattering to have such an eager model.

"Okay," Bess said. "Why not? I just need to mix up some paints and pick out my brushes."

Dulcie positively fluttered with glee.

From her box, Bess pulled out jars, each filled with a different color of paint powder: green, blue, black, gold. She decided to start with the chestnut powder, which was remarkably close to the shade of Dulcie's hair. She poured a small mound onto a piece of glass and added linseed oil. Then she carefully used her

palette knife to fold the two together. Soon she had a smooth chocolaty brown paste.

She mixed a few more colors and scooped them onto her palette. Pleased, she pulled a clean paintbrush from her pocket. Then she took a hard look at her model. Bess frowned.

"Dulcie," she said, "I wonder if maybe you could move around a little."

"Move around?" said Dulcie. "But what if I drop my rolls?"

And just then, a knock sounded at the door.

3

BESS OPENED HER DOOR to find an enormous bouquet of flowers. Two dainty feet in violet-petal shoes poked out below.

"Rosetta? Is that you?" Bess asked.

"Yes, it's me," replied a muffled voice from behind the flowers. Rosetta's pretty face peeked out from the side. "I brought you these," she said. With a groan, she heaved the heavy bunch toward Bess.

"Lily of the valley. My favorite! What a nice surprise, Rosetta!" Bess exclaimed.

Bess managed to drop the flowers into her cockleshell umbrella stand. She knocked over a few paint pots and canvases as she did.

"I thought you'd like them." Rosetta beamed. "In fact, I thought you might enjoy *painting* them. Or perhaps it would be better for you if I posed *with* them! As if I were walking through my garden, you know? Something like this—"

Pointing her nose in the air, Rosetta rose on one toe and struck a dramatic pose. "Luckily, I just had my hair done. Usually it's such a mess. Make sure you

get each curl, now. Oh, this is going to look so great in my room!"

Bess was speechless. "Er . . ."

"What Bess is trying to say," Dulcie called from across the room, "is that we are already in the middle of a painting." She held up her basket of rolls for Rosetta to see. "As we say in the kitchen, 'First fairy to come, first fairy served!' But don't worry. Bess will let you know when she's done with *my* portrait. Won't you, Bess?"

"Er . . . ," said Bess.

"Oh, I see," Rosetta said. Her delicate wings slumped sadly. "Well, in the meantime, I'll go clear a space back in my room for my new portrait. I know exactly where it should go!" She gave them both a little wave and hurried out.

"Fly safely!" called Dulcie.

Bess closed the door behind Rosetta. She felt extremely flattered— and still a little stunned. It was part of her role as an art talent to do paintings for her fellow fairies. Till that morning, they had always been for special occasions: an Arrival Day portrait, or a new painting for the Home Tree corridor. In between, she was as free as a bird to paint whatever she wanted.

But now, right out of the blue, *two* fairies wanted their pictures painted in one day! That was a record for any art-talent fairy, Bess was sure.

Bless my wings, she thought. *Who knew*

that Never fairies had such great taste!

"Shall we continue?" asked Dulcie.

Bess picked up her brush and nodded. "Of course!"

But within minutes, another knock sounded at the door . . . then another . . . and another!

By midday, fifteen fairies had paid Bess a visit, and fourteen wanted their portraits painted. (Terence, a dust-talent sparrow man, had stopped by only to drop off Bess's daily portion of fairy dust and to compliment her on Tinker Bell's portrait.)

Everyone wanted a portrait just like Tink's. There were so many requests, in fact, that Bess had given up on painting them one at a time. Instead, she had each fairy come in to sit for a sketch. Her plan was to finish the paintings later. But by the fourteenth fairy, even finishing a sketch began to look iffy.

"Fern, it's really hard to sketch you when you keep dusting my paper," Bess said to the dusting-talent fairy hovering over her easel.

"Oops!" said Fern. She darted back to the pedestal Bess had set up for her. "It's a habit," she explained. "But *really*, Bess." She shook her head. "I do wish you'd let a dusting talent in here once in a while! How can you stand it? And now, with all these baskets and flowers . . . my goodness! It's a forest of dust-catchers!"

It was true. Bess's studio was even more cluttered than usual. Fairies who'd come hoping for portraits had brought gifts. There were berries and walnuts from the harvest-talent fairies, cheeses from the dairy-talent fairies, and baskets upon baskets of goodies from the talents in the kitchen. Then there were more baskets from the grass-weaving talents. Not to mention a bubbling foot-high fountain from Silvermist, the water-talent fairy.

Luckily, not all fairies had come with gifts. Hairdressing, floor-polishing, and window- and wing-washing fairies had come offering their services. One music-talent fairy even played a song she'd written just for Bess. (To Bess's dismay, it was *still* stuck in her head!)

"Oh!" Fern exclaimed suddenly.

"There's a speck on your pencil there! Hold on!" She examined it. "Looks like pollen." Then another grain caught her eye. "Over there by the door! Fairy dust. I'll bet Terence left that one."

Feather duster waving at full speed, Fern darted about the room. Bess tried her best to sketch the fairy in action.

At least this is the last sketch I have to do, Bess told herself. *Then just fourteen portraits to paint . . .*

Knock-knock-knock.

Bess's stomach did a backflip. *Again?* For a second, she was tempted to pretend that no one was home. But she quickly realized that Fern's darting glow and humming duster had already given them away.

Slowly, Bess opened the door.

"Oh, Quill! It's you!" Bess let out a sigh of relief that even Fern could hear. "You wouldn't believe how many fairies and sparrow men have come to my studio today," she said.

She tried not to sound boastful. But she wanted Quill to know how much the other fairies liked her work. Bess always felt self-conscious around Quill. Perhaps it was because Quill was so unbelievably neat, while Bess was so messy.

"Fourteen!" Bess blurted, unable to hold back. "Everyone wanting portraits! I've never seen anything like it!" she went on. "I mean, just look at all the things they've brought me!" She waved her brush at the piles of gifts. Then suddenly she paused. "You weren't coming to ask for a portrait, too, were you?"

The art-talent fairy shook her head and smiled. "No, I just came by to see if you were ready to go to lunch. I've heard they're serving mushroom tarts and buttercup soup!"

Buttercup soup! Bess hadn't had that in ages, it seemed. *Mmm*—she could taste it already. Then her eyes fell on the pile of sketches on her table.

"I can't." She sighed. "Everyone is counting on me to finish the portraits as soon as I can. I've never seen fairies so passionate about art." She glanced at Quill out of the corner of her eye. "My portrait of Tinker Bell really touched them. *Deeply!* Mushroom tarts and buttercup soup will simply have to wait."

Bess sighed again. "It's hard to be so important. But I am up to the challenge—and I won't let Pixie Hollow down! Please give the other art talents my greetings, though, won't you, Quill?"

Quill was about to respond when Fern suddenly poked her head out from behind the birch-bark cabinet.

"Did you say buttercup soup?" she asked. "Hang on, Quill. I'm coming with you!"

She flew across the room, swiping at a few dust grains along the way. "Let me know when my portrait's done, Bess. Oooh! I cannot wait to dust it!" she said brightly.

Bess watched the fairies go, and she shut the door behind them. She looked at the sketch she had *tried* to do of Fern. It wasn't perfect, but it was fine for a sketch, she decided. *And it's probably a good idea to start painting now,* Bess thought. *I have a lot to do!*

Filled with a sense of duty, Bess churned out several portraits in the next few hours. But when she started the portrait of Rosetta, the garden-talent fairy—who had *insisted* on wearing her best rose-petal outfit—Bess froze.

Oh, no!

She couldn't believe it. She was all out of red paint! She couldn't finish Rosetta's portrait without it!

There was just one thing to do: go out and get more. This emergency called for berry juice—and lots of it.

Bess picked up a piece of paper and one of her best calligraphy twigs. She wrote a sign and hung it on her door:

Out to get more paint.
Please come back later.

Bess

Then she grabbed one of Dulcie's rolls, along with the first basket she could find, and flew out into the warm afternoon.

4

THE CURRANT ORCHARD was not far from Bess's studio. It was just across Havendish Stream.

Currant juice was a cheerful bright red, which would make fine paint, Bess knew. As she flew toward the fruits, they looked so pretty that Bess had an urge to paint them right then and there. Ah, but how could she? So many fairies were waiting for their portraits. She couldn't disappoint them.

Bess flitted from branch to branch. She piled as many plump currants into her basket as she could carry. A basketful would be—she hoped—enough for now.

She placed one last fruit atop her wobbly pile, then reached out and picked one for herself. If she couldn't paint the currants, at least she could taste them!

She licked her lips, then took a big hungry bite. The sweet red juice dribbled down her chin. Bess watched it fall, drip by drip, onto her skirt. It mixed with paint splatters there.

She swiped at her chin with the back of her hand. *Yes!* she thought with satisfaction. *This color will do just fine!*

When she was done eating, Bess grabbed hold of the basket's handle. She stretched up her wings, ready to fly away. The heavy basket, however, was not going anywhere. Bess could pick it up— just barely. But she couldn't carry it more than an inch at a time.

She tried unloading a few currants, but it didn't help much. And if she took

out too many, she wouldn't have enough to make paint when she got home.

Enviously, Bess watched a bluebird soaring overhead. If only she could speak to animals, like an animal-talent fairy, maybe she could get some help. But she couldn't even tell the gnats hovering around to go away. No matter how hard she shooed, they just kept returning.

"Oh, well," Bess said with a sigh. "I guess an inch at a time will have to do."

Bess flew—or hopped, really—out of the orchard and back toward her studio. By the time she reached Havendish Stream, she had settled into a comfortable rhythm: *flap, flap, flap, flap-jump-land. Flap, flap, flap, flap-jump-land.* But the crystal-clear stream stopped her short.

It wasn't that Havendish Stream was very big; a young deer could have crossed it in a single leap. To a fairy, however, it was huge. And there wasn't a bridge. Fairies usually just flew over the stream.

What am I going to do now? thought Bess. The stream was too wide to hop across. And though she didn't mind getting her feet and legs wet, she didn't want to risk getting her wings wet, too. Water soaked into fairy wings, as into a sponge. And if the stream was deep enough, waterlogged wings could drag her under.

Still, Bess had gotten this far. She wasn't going to give up now!

She thought for a moment. Then she picked up one of the plump currants.

With a mighty heave, she tossed it across the stream. The currant landed with a soft bounce on the moss on the other side.

Bess cheered, then reached for another. Soon she was tossing currants across the stream one after the other.

When her basket was empty, Bess lifted it effortlessly and flew across the stream. Then she refilled it and set off hopping once more. She was quite pleased with her clever solution.

"Now to make some paint!"

Back at her studio, Bess dragged a well-worn coconut shell from its resting place against her crate. She set it on the grass next to the back wall and dumped her basketful of currants into it.

Normally, Bess made her paints in small batches. But she'd spent far more time collecting the currants than she'd planned. If she was ever going to get all those fairies their portraits, she'd have to start speeding things up—a lot! That meant making *lots* of paint.

Bess kicked off her shoes and rolled up her spider-silk leggings. Then, ever so carefully, she climbed into the shell.

"Oops!" Bess slipped and almost fell. She caught herself on the shell.

POP! Squish! The pulpy fruit burst out of its skin and oozed coolly between her toes. Bess stomped around in the bowl. Her feet moved faster and faster.

She tried her best to keep her wings high and dry. But she could tell they were growing heavy with juice. *No matter,* she thought. *They'll have plenty of time to dry while I paint.* She looked down at the ruby red juice in the shell. Her heart filled with joy. Without thinking about it, she began to sing. . . .

"Oh, *fairy, fairy, fly with me—*"

"Bess? What are you doing?"

The voice behind Bess took her by surprise. She wavered, and her foot slipped.

Splash!

Bess fell face-first into the sticky red currant mash.

"Bess?"

Slowly, Bess reached for the edge of the shell and pulled herself up. Peeking

over the side, she saw Quill's pretty face staring back. In Quill's hands was a tray full of dishes covered with acorn caps.

"Are you all right?" Quill asked.

"Perfectly fine," said Bess. She spit out a bit of currant. "I'm just—uh—making some paint for all my portraits."

Inwardly, Bess groaned. Why did Quill always catch her in her messiest moment?

With as much dignity as she could manage, Bess pulled herself out of the shell. She tumbled to the ground. Covered in bright red juice, she looked as if she had a very bad sunburn.

"I brought you some dinner," Quill said. She set down the tray. "You need a hot meal to keep up your strength."

Even through the currant juice, Bess could smell the rich scents coming from the dishes. She wished, more than anything, that Quill hadn't seen her this way. But it was hard not to be grateful for such a kind gesture.

"I know I'll enjoy it," Bess said.

"Would you like some help washing your wings?" Quill asked. Her tone was sincere. But Bess caught the corners of her mouth turning up in a smile.

Bess shook her head and blushed. "Oh, no," she assured Quill. "I'll get to that . . . when I can."

"As you wish," Quill replied. She fluttered her wings and turned back toward the Home Tree.

5

DESPITE HER EMBARRASSMENT, Bess enjoyed
the dinner Quill had brought. And she
hoped it would give her more energy to
work.

But painting wasn't easy. The currant
juice quickly dried into a sticky sap. It
made Bess's hair and clothes stiff and
her wings all but useless.

If I'm ever going to get more painting

done, Bess thought, *I'll have to clean myself up.*

She set off toward Havendish Stream again. Her wings were too stiff now for her even to hop, so instead she walked through the meadow. Unfortunately, because fairies hardly ever walked, there were no paths to follow.

Bess climbed through the grass, in and out of a bush, and through a patch of dandelions. By the time she reached the stream, she could hardly move for all the grass and seeds and fluff sticking to her.

She made her way down the mossy bank to the shore. And then she stopped. How was she going to do this?

Bess knew she should have put aside her pride and let Quill help her wash her wings. It wasn't an easy job for any fairy to do by herself. But at the time, Bess had just wanted Quill to leave.

So now the problem was, what if she fell into the water? She had no idea how deep the water was. But she could see that the stream was running at an impish, happy-to-knock-you-over-and-carry-you-away pace.

Cautiously, she dipped in a toe.

"Ooh!" It was cold!

Still, Bess had little choice. It was much too far to walk back to the Home Tree for a proper bath. So she knelt beside the stream. Cupping her hands, she began to splash water onto herself to try to wash the grass and juice away.

The dried juice in her hair was

particularly hard to wash out. Finally, she gave up splashing. She leaned over, ready to stick her whole head in the water.

Crrrooaak!

A frog Bess hadn't noticed leaped into the stream. It landed with a splash. Bess didn't have a chance of keeping her balance. The next thing she knew, she fell headfirst into the water, making quite a splash of her own.

"Sppplugh!"

She kicked and waved and sputtered, even though her bottom was firmly on the stream's pebbled floor. Luckily, the water was not very deep. Yet the harder Bess flailed, the faster the playful stream became. At last it began to carry her away!

"Stop! Let me out!" Bess begged.

By then her wings were impossibly heavy. "Help!" Bess cried. "Help! Help! *Help!*"

"Bess!" a voice called out. "Stop kicking! The stream doesn't like it! Just calm down, and I'll pull you out. What were you *doing?*"

Bess made herself relax. A second later, her friend Rani, a water-talent fairy, pulled her out of the water. Bess was safe, if sopping, on a sandy shore.

"Rani, you saved me!" Bess panted, as much with exhaustion as with relief. "You must let me do something for you." She tried to raise herself onto her elbows. But her waterlogged wings felt like weights on her back. She settled for rolling over to face her friend. "I know! How about a—"

"—portrait!" Rani almost shrieked. "Just like Tinker Bell's? Bess, you read our minds! We were just talking about how wonderful it would be for each of us to have a portrait!"

"Each of you?" Bess said, confused.

"Yes, each of us!" Rani replied. "Everyone," she called to a group of water-talent fairies. "Come down here and see Bess. She's going to paint portraits of all of us. We'll be the first talent group to have a complete set!" She teared up with joy. "And could somebody please bring me a leafkerchief?" she asked, sniffing loudly.

In seconds, a dozen eager water fairies surrounded Bess.

"So when can you get started?" Rani asked.

"Well, honestly," Bess began, "I have several others to finish first. And then I'll probably have to make more—"

"—paint!" Rani cut in knowingly. "Of course."

"I hope you'll use *watercolors* for all of our portraits," Silvermist said with a giggle. The whole group of water-talent fairies laughed.

Bess managed to smile politely. She struggled to her feet.

"Oh, here, let me help you," said Rani. "You'll never get anywhere with wings *that* full of water."

She brushed a bit of fairy dust from her arm onto Bess's wings. Then she held

her hands above them. Closing her eyes,
Rani drew the water out in a thin silvery
ribbon. She formed it into a ball and
tossed it into the stream.

"Your wings will still be damp for a while," she said, turning back to Bess. "But at least they won't weigh you down."

Bess stood and gave her wings a little flap. "Much better," she said with relief. But her relief turned to dismay as she thought of the new portraits . . . a whole *talent*'s worth. Goodness!

As she said good-bye to the water fairies, Bess tried to remind herself that portrait painting was an honor.

"Don't forget about our portraits!" the fairies called after her.

"Oh," said Bess, "I won't."

6

BESS HEADED BACK across the meadow, in the direction of her studio. To her dismay, her flying was a little wobbly since her wings were still a bit damp. *But at least I'm clean,* she thought. She tore off a piece of grass and used it to tie back a lock of hair.

With a sigh, Bess realized that she could use some clean clothes. She hadn't been back to her room in the Home Tree in quite a while. A bit of freshening up in general might do her some good. So she quickly turned away from her studio, toward the Home Tree.

As she neared the knothole door, however, her stomach began to churn. Bess's room was in the tree's south-southwest branch. That meant passing dozens of rooms and workshops. Who knew how many fairies she might meet along the way? And what if they all wanted portraits? Not that Bess didn't want to paint them all. She just wasn't sure she wanted to do it right *now*.

No, going through the Home Tree was *not* the way to get to her room, Bess decided. She would have to sneak in through her back window instead.

Bess had never flown to her room from behind before. But really, how hard could it be? She circled the trunk to the side where the low evening sun was shining. Thank goodness it hadn't set yet! Then she looked up at the rows of brightly colored window boxes along the tree's branches.

Now, that's a subject for painting, she thought wistfully. But right now, the window boxes were for counting.

"One . . . two . . . three . . . four . . . five . . ."

Bess got to thirteen, but then she had to stop. The Home Tree's leafy branches began to block her view. Bess flew closer and continued counting.

"Fourteen . . . fifteen . . . sixteen. Here it is!"

Funny, she thought, *I don't remember that leaf in front of my window.*

Bess flew over to the window and tugged on the sash. Stubbornly, it refused to give. She pulled a little harder. But still the window held fast.

"What am I going to do now?" Bess said. She balled her fists and pounded the window in frustration.

Immediately, the window gave way. Bess tumbled inside.

How odd, she thought, shaking her sore head. *I always thought that window opened out. . . .*

"Bess!" came an alarmed voice from across the room. "Are you all right?"

"Quill!" Bess cried, looking up. "What are you doing here?"

"I'm sculpting—in my room," Quill replied. Her voice now sounded more puzzled than shocked.

"*Your* room?" Bess bit her lip as she rose to her feet. Her eyes darted around the tidy chamber. She looked from one stone sculpture to another, over to the cast-bronze bedstead, and then to the marble busts set into each wall. Finally, her eyes went back to Quill.

"Yes," Quill said. "My room. Did you need something, Bess?"

Bess tried to swallow the lump in her throat. She choked out a laugh. "Need something! Ha! That's a good one, Quill. No. No. No. I was just . . .

er . . . flying by . . . to let you know I *don't* need anything! And, uh . . ." She looked down at her limp, wrinkled, stained skirt. "To show you that I cleaned up . . . all by myself!"

She swallowed once more and stretched her mouth into a grin.

"I see," said Quill. She still looked confused. "I'm . . . so glad."

"Anyway," Bess went on, "I have portraits of all the water-talent fairies to do. I really must fly off."

"Are you sure I can't help you in some way?" Quill asked again.

"Absolutely not," said Bess. Still grinning, she took a backward hop toward the door . . . and ran straight into a granite statue of a luna moth. With a crash it fell from its pedestal onto the hard wooden floor.

Bess cringed. "Oh, no!"

"Don't worry." Quill flew over and sprinkled some fairy dust on the heavy statue. Then she used the magic to stand it back up. "No harm done," she said.

"Truly," said Bess, "I'd fly backward if I could."

Quill laughed. "Flying backward is how you knocked it over in the first place."

Bess knew it was a joke. But she couldn't help noticing that Quill hovered protectively next to the moth statue.

Bess blushed. "See you later, Quill," she said. And she hurried out of the room before she could do more damage.

Oh, of all the rooms to fall into by mistake, why did it have to be Quill's? Bess thought as she flew to the next room down the hall. She reached for the knob. Then, just to be safe, she checked the number on the door to make sure it was hers.

Inside, Bess's mood quickly lifted. It was a relief to be among her favorite things.

She flew to her bed, which was covered in a multicolored quilt made from different kinds of flower petals. She lay back and gazed up at the stained-glass window above her. The sun was almost down, but there was just enough light to allow the colors to dance along the wall across the room.

And, oh, the walls! They were covered with framed pictures of every shape and size. Many were gifts from other art fairies. The rest were drawings and paintings that Bess had done herself. There was her very first sketch of Mother Dove. Next to it hung her Home Tree series. She'd followed the tree through all its seasons—spring and summer (which were the only seasons in Never Land).

Each work reminded Bess of a time and place and mood. Some were good and some were bad, but each was special in its own way.

Then her eyes fell on a statue in the corner. It was a portrait of Bess carved out of smooth sandalwood. Quill had given it to her as a gift on her last Arrival

Day anniversary. Quill had remembered how much more Bess liked wood than hard, cold stone.

Bess smiled at the statue. It was a perfect likeness, right down to Bess's long bangs and the paintbrush behind her ear.

Funny, Bess thought. She yawned and let her heavy eyelids close for just a moment. *If I didn't know better, I'd say that was the work of a good friend.*

7

The next thing she knew, Bess awoke to a loud knock at her door. She didn't even remember falling asleep! What time was it?

Knock-knock-knock.

"Bess! Are you in there?"

Groggily, Bess flew up and opened the door.

"Hi, Bess! It's me! Is it done?"

It was Dulcie.

"I went to your studio. Your sign said you'd be there this morning. But when you never showed up, I thought maybe I'd find you here."

"Oh," said Bess. She pushed her hair out of her eyes, trying to wake up.

"So?" Dulcie went on. "Is it done?"

"Is what done?"

"My portrait!"

"Oh!" Bess thought for a moment. "As a matter of fact, it is. But it's not here, of course. It's back at my studio."

"Well, come on!" Dulcie grabbed her arm. "Let's go!"

By the time they reached the tangerine crate, Bess was wide awake. She was pleased to be presenting the new portrait.

She had to admit, though, that she was a little disappointed that Dulcie hadn't brought another plate of rolls, or some other tasty treat.

"I came as soon as I woke up!" Dulcie explained excitedly, almost as if she could read Bess's thoughts. "I haven't even been to the kitchen yet to bake."

"Really?" Bess was touched. How important this was to Dulcie! "Let's take a look, then, shall we?" she said.

She led Dulcie to a row of easels, each draped with a thick velvet-moss cloth. With a quick flick of the wrist, and just the right touch of drama and modesty (something every art fairy arrives with), she yanked off the cover of the nearest one.

"Ooh!" Dulcie fluttered up and down. She clapped her hands. "I love it! I love it!" she gushed. "I can practically taste those poppy puff rolls right now!" And as if to test them, she reached out to touch the painting. Then she stopped.

"What? What is it?" asked Bess.

"Do my wings really stick up like that in back?" Dulcie asked. The joy slowly drained from her face.

"What do you mean?" said Bess.

"My wings!" said Dulcie. "They're . . . *huge*." She strained her neck, trying to see behind herself. "They're not really that big, are they?"

"Actually, they are," came a cheerful voice from just outside the door. "Good morning, Bess. Dulcie. Is my portrait ready, too?"

"Hello, Rosetta," replied Bess. She was still stunned by Dulcie's reaction. "Er, yes. Yours is done, too."

While Dulcie anxiously compared her wings with those in the painting, Bess reached for the second velvet cover and pulled it off.

Rosetta beamed. Then a tiny wrinkle formed between her brows.

"How do you like the lilies of the valley?" Bess asked. "I tried to make each one practically perfect, just like yours, but not so perfect that they wouldn't look real."

"Oh, yes, they're very nice," Rosetta said. Still, she looked concerned. "It's just . . . my *nose*. I know for a fact that it's much prettier than *that*."

Dulcie glanced away from her portrait. "Actually, it's not."

Rosetta frowned. "Yes, it is. Would you mind, Bess," she went on, "going back and straightening my nose . . . and maybe taking a little off the sides?"

"Oh, yes!" said Dulcie. "Could you make my wings smaller, too, Bess? That would be wonderful!"

Bess's mouth fell open. Every fairy had her opinions. But Bess had never before been asked to change her art. Like all talents, she prided herself on doing her best from the very beginning. What were these fairies thinking?

But Bess didn't even have time to reply before a dozen more fairies swooped into her studio, each one eager to see her brand-new portrait. And each one, Bess could tell, was eager to offer her honest opinion.

By the time the fairies had left, Bess was drained—and hungry.

She looked at the sun outside her window. It was high in the sky. She had probably missed breakfast by a good hour. But perhaps a few kind serving talents would still be serving tea.

Bess sure hoped so.

As soon as she reached the Home Tree, she flew straight through the lobby and down the long corridor to the tearoom.

She headed directly for the art-talent

fairies' table. As she had feared, the other art-talent fairies had finished their breakfast and returned to their own studios. Most of the tables in the tearoom were empty, in fact. The cleaning-talent fairies were busy taking dirty teacups and breakfast trays away.

"Bessy, dear!" called Laidel, a serving-talent fairy. She swooped up beside Bess. "We were afraid you weren't coming. Let me bring you some tea. And maybe a scone?"

"That would be lovely," said Bess, sinking into a chair.

"Coming right up!" said Laidel.

In moments, the fairy was back. Her tray was piled high with Bess's favorite tea, sweet cream and clover honey, heart-

shaped currant—*Ugh!* Bess thought—
scones, blueberry muffins with freshly
churned butter, and a tall stack of buckwheat pancakes dripping with warm
syrup.

"I thought you looked a bit tired,

Bess," said Laidel. "So I brought you a little extra." She gave Bess a wink as she poured a stream of tea into a cup. She set it down before Bess. "Don't tell the other fairies!"

Bess smiled at her gratefully and took a sip. "Ahh! Just what I needed."

"I'm so glad," said Laidel. "Now, just sit back, relax, and enjoy your tea. There you go. I'll come back in a little while and we can talk about my portrait."

Pwahhh! Bess's eyes popped open and the tea she'd been sipping sprayed across the tablecloth. Her cup fell to the floor, where the rest of the tea made a stain on the floral carpet.

Bess reached down to mop it up with her napkin. But another hand, clutching a springy moss sponge, beat her to it.

"Allow me," said Colin, a rather tall (in fairy terms) and rather plump (in any terms) cleaning-talent sparrow man. He dabbed at the spill until no trace of tea was left. Then he flew off with the empty cup and returned in an instant with a new one.

"If there's anything else I can do for you, Bess," he said with a bow, "let me know."

"I will," said Bess.

"For instance," Colin went on, "if you'd like me to pose for one of your portraits, just ask. I'm sure you don't come across a model like *me* every day!"

Bess shook her head. "Er, no, I don't," she said. "But to tell you the truth,

Colin, I don't need any more models today. I'm a little behind, I'm afraid."

"No problem," Colin said with a shrug. "We'll do it tomorrow." With a smile, he turned. "Hey, Elda!" he called to a cleaning-talent fairy across the room. "I talked to Bess. She says we should come by her studio *tomorrow!*"

Bess poured a new cup of tea. But the joy of the meal had gone away. Not even the buckwheat pancakes (which had always been Bess's favorite) tasted good.

Maybe I should leave, she thought. *I should get busy painting again. Besides, who knows how many more portraits I'll have to do if I stay!*

But it was too late. Suddenly, a whole

line of eager fairies flew out of the kitchen—baking talents, dish-washing talents, silver-polishing talents, serving talents, and everyone else who happened to be around.

"Hi, Bess," called Dulcie. "Colin said you were here. Did you like the scones? I told everyone in the kitchen about my portrait. And don't you know, now they all want one!"

"Oh, yes!" said another baking-talent fairy. "We've each got to have a portrait, too!"

Bess tried not to groan. But it hardly would have mattered if she had. The fairies were busy chattering with each other, describing *exactly* how they wanted their portraits to be.

"Just be sure to keep your wings tucked in," Dulcie said knowingly.

Finally, Bess held up her hands.

"Friends," she began, "I am truly, truly honored by your regard for my work. But I'm not sure I can paint all your portraits right now. Maybe a quick sketch would do?" she asked hopefully.

The fairies looked at one another.

"No," said one silver-polisher. "We want *portraits*, like everyone else."

"Yes!" the others chimed in. "We want portraits! We want portraits! We want portraits!"

8

Bess left the tearoom with sixteen more portraits to do.

She hoped she'd have enough paint. But as she pulled one, and then another, paintbrush from the pouch at her waist, she realized she would definitely need more brushes.

Vole hair made the best paintbrushes. Bess could usually find patches of it near the edge of the forest. (Those voles just shed like crazy.) The forest was not far from her studio. She decided that she should fly by and collect some on her way.

And she was so glad she did. The light was *gorgeous*! It was streaming through the trees, casting deep, dark shadows that were so . . . interesting!

Back to business, Bess reminded herself over and over.

But where were all the vole hairs?

Then, at last, just when Bess thought she would have to make do with dandelion fluff, she spotted a tuft of tiny gray hairs stuck to a blade of grass.

She darted over and began to collect them. All of a sudden, she felt a firm, sharp peck on the top of her head!

"Chrrrp-chrrrp! Trillillillillill!"

Bess spun around to see a stern gray bird staring at her. It was twice as big as she was.

"Eeeek!" shrieked Bess.

"Eeeek!" chirped the bird. *"Chrrr-chrrr-chrrrp-trrrillll!"*

A voice rose from the shadows. "She says she needs those hairs for her nest."

Bess looked to the right and saw a reddish brown head poke out from behind a short stump.

"Fawn," Bess said, "I'd fly backward if I could. I didn't know."

"That's okay," Fawn replied. She was an animal-talent fairy. She could talk to animals in their own languages. "These mockingbirds are a little testy.

But they don't mean any harm. Just looking out for their babies."

Bess rubbed the sore spot on her head. "I see." She watched the bird pluck the hairs with her beak.

"Do you think she could spare a few hairs for a new paintbrush?" Bess asked Fawn.

Fawn grinned and turned to the bird. Together, they twittered and chirped for a good three or four minutes. Then the fairy turned back to Bess and nodded.

"Take as many as you need," Fawn said.

"That's kind of her!" said Bess. "What in Never Land did you say?"

Fawn grinned again. "I just told her what a fantastic and famous fairy artist you are. And that you needed hairs for a new paintbrush. *And* that if she shared hers, you would paint her portrait!" She winked at Bess and whispered, "She's quite vain, you know. Oh, and I also told her you would paint me, too."

"Paint you?" said Bess.

"Would you?" asked Fawn. "Everyone is talking about your portraits, and I've never had one done. I just saw Madge's. I don't care how much she thinks she looks like a dragonfly—I think it's wonderful! What a great talent you have! Tell me"—Fawn paused and wrapped her arms fondly around the bird—"do you want to paint us here? Or back at your studio?"

"Right now?" Bess said.

"Why not?" said Fawn with a shrug.

"It's early. Besides," she went on with a nod toward the mockingbird, "it's the only way you're going to get your vole hairs."

With a halfhearted sigh, Bess sank onto a patch of moss. She pulled some pencils and her sketchbook from her smock. "I'll *sketch* you here," she told the eager pair. "Then I'll paint you back at my studio. *Alone*."

The mockingbird warbled something to Fawn. "Be sure to paint her right side—it's her best," Fawn translated. "See, what did I tell you? Oh! And when you do me, don't feel as if you have to make my teeth so big, you know? There are some fairies who call me Chipmunk. Can you believe it?"

Bess began her sketch, just as she'd done for all the fairies.

But she soon found her interest drifting away from her models and off to the forest.

The sun slowly shifted across the late-morning sky. A gentle breeze swept up and blew a flock of woolly clouds across the blue horizon. Closer to the forest's edge, shadows shivered and danced about on the ground.

And then, the west wind kicked in. At first, it was refreshing. But Never winds are fickle and prone to mischief, especially those from the west. And this one was no different.

It began by blowing all the dandelions' fluff off their stalks, leaving their bald-headed stems to flap about. Then it moved into the trees. It worked the leaves into a rustling frenzy. It sent acorns and hickory nuts crashing to the ground.

Feathers flying, the mockingbird did her best to hold her ground—and her good side. Fawn clung to her neck with all her might.

"Uh, Bess! Shall we call it a day?" Fawn hollered over the din.

"Hold on!" Bess called back. She was sketching furiously in her book. "I'm almost done."

"I *can't* hold on!" Fawn cried.

The mockingbird let out a stream of frantic chirps. The wind gleefully carried away half of them. But Fawn understood.

"She has to get back to her nest, Bess," Fawn shouted. "Crazy wind! Her babies are scared!"

Bess sighed. Fawn was right. They all should go. Besides, by now it wasn't easy to keep her sketchbook from blowing away.

She said good-bye to the mockingbird, who swiftly flew off to her chicks. Fawn asked a chipmunk to carry her and Bess home. And off they rode. Bess held her book of sketches tightly. Her heart was full of newfound joy.

Then the wind died away.

9

Bess couldn't wait to start painting!

She was bursting with inspiration. Her brushes flew about the canvas.

It wasn't until she stepped back from it that Bess realized that what she had painted wasn't a portrait at all. It was the forest, as she had seen it, in all its pinwheels of texture and color. Great swirls of greens and blues, whites and browns, bright yellows and mysterious grays filled her canvas.

Oh, but it was satisfying! So full of energy and life. Bess hadn't felt this good since she'd finished Tink's portrait. *What's the difference?* she wondered. *What has been missing from all my paintings lately?*

Bess left her studio and flew toward the Home Tree. On her way, she saw a message-talent fairy. Bess stopped her.

"Do you think you could ask everyone to gather in the courtyard today, just before teatime?" Bess asked her. "The light should be perfect for the unveiling of my newest painting! It's a masterpiece!"

"Of course," the message-talent fairy said, and she quickly flew off.

Bess counted the minutes until teatime. And she couldn't help staring at the masterpiece. Any fairy who appreciated fine painting would absolutely *love* it! She was sure.

Bess's new painting was quite large by fairy standards—five by seven inches. She sprinkled it with fairy dust to make it easier to carry. Then she covered it with a piece of silky cloth and set off for the courtyard of the Home Tree.

Bess had planned on being the first fairy to arrive. But to her surprise, the courtyard was practically full. Everyone was eager to see Bess's great masterpiece.

"It might be a portrait of me!" a

dust-talent fairy told a water-talent fairy.

"Or it might be of Fawn," said an animal-talent fairy. "I heard that Bess wouldn't stop sketching her this morning—despite a windstorm!"

"I don't know," someone else said. "It's so large. Perhaps it's *all* of us!"

Finally, it was time. Bess flew up to call everyone to order. Her glow was practically white with excitement.

She smiled at the crowd. "I think you will be glad you flew here today . . . especially considering what art lovers you all have become! It is because you appreciate art that I couldn't wait to share my newest painting with you. And so . . ." Bess grabbed the cloth. She yanked it away with a flourish. "I call it . . . *Swept Away!*"

In the courtyard, there was silence.

Bess looked happily at her painting. Then she turned to her fans. But the faces staring back at her were blank.

"That's not *me*," she heard one or two fairies mumble.

"That's not me, either," echoed several more.

"No, of course!" Bess chuckled. "It's not any of you. It's . . . it's a feeling I had of being swept away! In the forest . . . in the moment . . . in my art! Isn't it wonderful?"

"It's *what?*" she heard Fawn call out.

"It's a feeling," Bess repeated.

Honestly! Bess's forehead wrinkled in frustration. She began to explain once more—but before she could say another word, the tea chimes rang.

"Teatime!" called Laidel.

"We're coming," several fairies cried in reply.

"Very nice, Bess," said a few water-talent fairies politely as they flew by. Bess looked for tears of emotion. But their eyes were surprisingly dry.

The other art-talent fairies applauded her. But even they seemed more eager than usual to make their way inside.

"Wait!" Bess meekly called. Where were all the adoring fairies? Where were all the requests for paintings of their own? Fiddlesticks! Where were all the compliments Bess had . . . well . . . gotten used to?

Within minutes, the courtyard was empty. Bess's glow faded from white to a dull, disappointed mustard color.

She felt her chin begin to tremble. Her eyes welled up with tears.

"Darling, I sincerely hope you're not *crying*. Don't we get enough of that with those pitiful water-talent fairies?"

Bess sniffled and looked up. She saw Vidia flying over.

"I'm not in the mood for your comments right now, Vidia," she managed to say, despite the lump in her throat.

"Suit yourself," said the fairy, turning to go. "I really didn't want to tell you anyway that I liked your painting."

"You *what?*" Bess said with a gasp.

"I like it," replied Vidia, looking back over her shoulder. "And I'd appreciate it, sweetheart, if you didn't make me say it again."

"Wait!" Bess called out. "Don't go! Stay!" She watched in amazement as the fairy zipped back toward her. "So you really like it?"

Vidia rolled her eyes. "Yes," she said.

Bess grinned. "*Ah*. At least someone does."

"Why, Bess, dear, don't you like it?"

"Well . . ." Bess stopped to consider Vidia's question. "Yes, I do. I like it very much."

"So there you are. Of course, I can see why you would value *my* opinion. But do you really care so much what those silly slowpokes think?" Vidia scoffed. "Really. And here I thought you were an artist."

It was hard to agree with someone as

unpleasant as Vidia. *But she has a point,* Bess thought. Bess loved her painting, and she'd loved painting it. And wasn't that really what art was all about? How could she have let herself forget so easily?

"Um, Vidia," she said. Her hands nervously twisted the cloth that had covered her painting. "Would you, by any chance, like to have this painting?"

For a split second, Vidia actually looked pleased. But her pale face quickly hardened into a scowl. "Darling, are you giving me a present?" she said haughtily. "What in Never Land have I ever done for *you?*"

"You told me the truth," Bess replied. "But more than that, my painting reached you. So I want you to have it."

Vidia's cold eyes moved from Bess to the enormous canvas. And Bess could see them faintly warming.

"I'll take good care of it," Vidia said finally. Then she took a pinch of fairy dust from the pouch hanging from her belt and sprinkled it onto the painting. Picking the painting up, she darted away.

Smiling, Bess watched her go. Then she took a deep breath and braced herself for the difficult task ahead.

10

BESS COULD SMELL the freshly baked honey buns and butter cookies even before she got to the tearoom. But that day, tea would have to wait until after her announcement.

She hated to think about how the other fairies would react. The best thing to do, she told herself, was not think too hard—just do it.

She flew to the front of the great room. She stood between the wide floor-to-ceiling windows and flapped her wings for attention.

"Everyone!" she called. "Everyone! I have an announcement."

The clink of china and the hum of voices, however, did not grow any fainter.

"I *said*," Bess shouted, "I have an important announcement to make!"

One of her wings accidentally knocked over a tea tray. At last, someone took notice.

"Oh, fairies!" Laidel called out. She clinked a spoon against a cup. "I think Bess has something to say."

The noise died down. All eyes turned to Bess.

"Uh . . ." Bess was suddenly nervous. How was she going to do this? She wished that she had written her announcement down.

"I . . . I just wanted to tell you all that I realized something important this morning—something I somehow let myself forget." She brushed her bangs out of her eyes. "The joy of my talent comes not *just* from painting, you see. It comes from painting what *inspires* me, *when* it inspires me. I think that is something you all can understand. I must be true to my talent, and to myself. And so"— Bess drew a deep breath—"although it has been a great honor to be asked to paint so many of your portraits, I won't be able to finish them for quite a while."

Bess closed her eyes. She waited for the backlash.

Clink, clank, slurrrp.

Bess slowly opened one eye, and then the other. All around the room, the fairies had gone back to their tea.

"Wait!" Bess blurted out. "Did you all hear what I said?"

"Oh, yes," several fairies replied.

"We sure did," said a few more.

"You need to be inspired," Laidel said. "We completely understand."

"I know!" said Dulcie, flying by with a plate of fresh rolls. "Maybe you'd be inspired by Hem's new dress! Stand up, Hem, and show her!"

A plump-cheeked, white-haired fairy modestly stood up. She modeled her

frock made of soft pink peony petals. It was tight in the waist and full down to the knees. Hem wore open-toed pink slippers dyed to match. Although Bess liked clothes that were more flowy and colorful, she had to agree that it was very nice.

"Oh, isn't it gorgeous!" cooed Rosetta from the table next to her.

"I've got to have one!" said another garden-talent fairy.

"Me too!" more fairies chimed in.

"Me first, though!" said Dulcie. "Hem promised to make one for me first. Didn't you, Hem? First fairy to come, first fairy served!"

Soon a ring four fairies deep had formed around poor Hem. Teatime— and Bess—had been forgotten.

Bess sank into a nearby chair. She stared, bewildered, at the scene. Could it be that Bess and her portraits had lost all their importance? Had she awakened any real art appreciation in the fairies? Or had her art been just a . . . just a *fad*?

The idea made her wings limp. Bess's spirits sank. Oh, the horror!

She buried her head in her arms, in case a tear should fall.

"Bess?"

She felt a cool hand on her shoulder.

"Why don't you come to our table?"

Slowly, Bess looked up into Quill's eyes. Her spirits sank even lower. As if making a complete fool of herself weren't bad enough. Did she have to do it right in front of Quill *again*?

"I saved you two star-shaped butter cookies. But if you don't eat them quickly, Linden will."

Bess sniffled a little and shook her head. "I'm not hungry," she said. "I don't know if I'll ever be hungry again."

"Oh, yes, you will," Quill said.

Bess pushed back her bangs. She sniffled once more. "How can you be so sure?"

"Because—" Quill began.

But before she could finish, she was interrupted by Hem's high-pitched voice from the far end of the room. "One at a time, fairies! Please! One at a time!"

Bess and Quill looked over at the ever-widening circle around the dressmaking fairy. They couldn't help smiling at each other.

Quill leaned toward Bess. "Remind me to tell you about the time, a few years before you arrived, when all the fairies decided they just *had* to have their very own tiny hand-carved talent symbols to wear around their necks."

"Really?" Bess was surprised. "That sounds lovely! But . . . I don't think I've ever seen one."

Quill grinned and nodded. "Exactly."

"*Ah!*" It took a moment, but Bess got it. "Fairies!"

Maybe I will have a cookie or two after all, Bess thought. And maybe she *would* paint Hem's cute pink dress. Perhaps with a bright green background! Or should it be orange? Or maybe she'd paint something else that day. Or do something with clay? She could even carve with Quill.

There was one thing for sure, though. From then on, whatever Bess did, it would be her choice—and hers alone.